Summer

James H. Schmitz

Alpha Editions

This edition published in 2024

ISBN : 9789364736275

Design and Setting By
Alpha Editions
www.alphaedis.com
Email - info@alphaedis.com

Summer Guests

By JAMES H. SCHMITZ

*No birds were these, and surely not of
a feather, and there was no need to tell
Mel by the company he kept—it told him!*

All through that Saturday night, rain drummed down mercilessly and unseasonably on Sweetwater Beach. Thunder pealed and lightning flared. In between, Mel Armstrong heard the steady boom of the Pacific surf not a block from his snug little duplex apartment. Mel didn't mind any of it. He was in bed, slightly swacked and wholly comfortable. He dozed, and now and then woke up far enough to listen admiringly to the racket.

At nine A. M., when he opened his eyes once more, he discovered the room was full of summer sunshine. Beyond his window gleamed a cloudless sky, and only the occasional gusts of wind indicated there had been anything like a storm during the night.

An exceptionally beautiful Sunday morning—made more beautiful, perhaps, by the fact that it marked the beginning of Mel Armstrong's annual two-week paid vacation. Mel was a salesman for Marty's Fine Liquors, a wholesale house. He was twenty-eight and in fairly good shape, but his job bored him. This morning, for the first time in months, he was fully aware of that. Perhaps it was the weather. At any rate, he had a sense, almost a premonition, of new and exciting events approaching him rapidly. Events that would break down the boundaries of his present humdrum existence and pitch him into the life of romantic adventure that, somehow, he seemed to have missed so far....

Recognizing this as a day-dream, but unwilling to give it up completely, Mel breakfasted unhurriedly in his pajamas. Then, struck by a sudden, down-to-earth suspicion, he stuck his head out of his living room window.

As he'd guessed, there were other reminders of the storm in the narrow courtyard before the window. Branches and assorted litter had blown in, including at least one soggily dismembered Sunday paper. The low rent he paid for his ground-floor apartment in the Oceanview Courts was based on an understanding with the proprietor that he and the upstairs occupant of the duplex would keep the court clean. The other five duplexes that fronted on the court were bulging with vacationing visitors from the city, which made it a real chore in summer.

Unfortunately, he couldn't count on his upstairs neighbor, a weird though rather amiable young character who called herself Maria de Guesgne. Maria went in for painting abstractions, constructing mobiles, and discussing the works of Madame Blavatsky. She avoided the indignity of manual toil.

Mel made himself decent by exchanging his pajamas for swimming trunks. Then he got a couple of brooms and a hose out of a garage back of the court and went to work.

He'd cleared the courtyard by the time the first of the seasonal guests began to show up in their doorways, and went on to inspect another, narrower court behind his duplex, which was also his responsibility. There he discovered Maria de Guesgne propped on her elbows on her bedroom window sill, talking reproachfully to a large gray tomcat that was sitting in the court. Both turned to look at Mel.

"Good morning, Mel!" Maria said, with unusual animation. She had long black bangs which emphasized her sallow and undernourished appearance.

"Morning," Mel replied. "Scat!" he added to the cat, which belonged to somebody else in the neighborhood but was usually to be found stalking about the Oceanview Courts.

"You shouldn't frighten poor Cat," said Maria. "Mel, would you look into the bird box?"

"Bird box?"

"The one in the climbing rose," said Maria, leaning precariously from the window to point. "To your left. Cat was trying to get at it."

The bird box was a white-painted, weather-beaten little house set into a straggly rose bush that grew out of a square patch of earth beside Mel's bedroom window. The box was about ten feet above the ground.

Mel looked up at it.

"I'm sure I heard little birds peeping in it this morning!" Maria explained sentimentally.

"No bird in its senses would go into a thing like that," Mel assured her. "I don't hear anything. And besides—"

"Please, Mel! We don't want Cat to get them!"

Mel groaned, got a wobbly step-ladder out of the garage and climbed up. The gray cat walked over and sat down next to the ladder to watch him.

He poked at the box and listened. No sound.

"Can't you open the top and look in?" Maria inquired.

Holding the box in one hand, Mel tentatively inserted his thumbnail into a crack under its top and pushed. The weathered wood splintered away easily.

"Don't break it!" Maria cried.

Mel put his eye to the crack he'd made. Then he gasped, jerked back, letting go of the box, teetered wildly a moment and fell over with the step-ladder. The cat fled, spitting.

"Oh, my!" said Maria, apparently with some enjoyment. "Poor Mel! Are you hurt?"

Mel stood up slowly. The bright morning world seemed to be spinning gently around him, but it wasn't because of his fall. "Of course not," he said. His voice quavered somewhat.

"Oh?" said Maria. "Well, then—*are* there any little birds in the nest?"

Mel swallowed hard. "No," he said. He bent over and carefully picked up the ladder and placed it against the wall. The action made it unnecessary to look at her.

"Eggs?" she asked in a hopeful tone.

"No eggs either! No nothing!" His voice was steady again, but he had to get rid of Maria. "Well, I'll clean up this court now, I guess. Uh—maybe you'd like to come down and lend a hand?"

Maria replied promptly that she certainly would like to, but she hadn't had breakfast yet; and with that she vanished from the window.

Mel looked round stealthily. The cat was watching from the door of the garage, but no one else was in sight.

Hurriedly, he replaced the step-ladder under the bird nest and climbed up again.

Setting the box carefully down on the table in his living room, he locked the apartment door and closed the Venetian blinds. All this had been done in a sort of quiet rush, as if every second counted, which it did in a way. Mel wasn't going to believe, even for a moment, that what he thought he'd seen in that box could be really there; and he couldn't disprove it fast enough to suit him. But something warned him that he wouldn't want to have any witnesses around when he did take his second look.

Then, as he turned from the window, he heard a thin piping cry, a voice as tiny as the peeping of a mouse, coming from the table, from the box.

An instant fright reaction froze him where he stood. The sounds stopped again. There was a brief, faint rustle, like the stirring of dry parchment, and then quiet.

The rustling, he thought, must have been the wings—he'd been *sure* they had wings. Otherwise—

It could all have been an illusion, he told himself. An illusion that transformed a pair of featherless nestlings into something he still didn't want to give a name to. Color patterns of jade and pink flashed into his memory next, however, which made the bird theory shaky. Say a rather small green-and-pink snake then, or a lizard—

Except, of course, for the glassy glitter of the wings. So make it instead, Mel thought desperately, a pair of big insects, like dragonflies, only bigger....

He shook his head and moistened his lips. That wouldn't explain that tiny voice—and the more he tried to rationalize it all, the more scared he was getting. Assume, he took the mental jump, he really had seen the figures of two tiny, naked, green-and-pink people in there—with wings! One didn't have to drag in the supernatural to explain it. There were things like flying saucers, presumably, and probably such beings might exist on other worlds.

The thought was oddly reassuring. He still felt as if he'd locked himself in the room with things potentially in the class of tarantulas, but there was excitement and wonder coming up now. With a surge of jealous proprietorship, he realized that he didn't want to share this discovery with anybody else. Later, perhaps. Right now, it was *his* big adventure.

The room was too dim to let him distinguish anything inside the box as he had outdoors, and he was still reluctant to get his face too close to it. He gave it a gingerly rap with his knuckle and waited. No sound.

He cleared his throat. "Hello?" he said. Immediately, that seemed like an idiotic approach. Worse than that, it also brought no reaction.

For the first time, Mel had a sense of worry for the occupants of the box. There was no way of guessing how they'd got in there, but they might be sick or dying. Hurriedly he brought a lamp over to the table and tried to direct light inside, both through the round hole in its side and through the opening he'd made in the top. It wasn't very effective and produced no stir within.

With sudden decision, he shoved one hand into the opening, held the box with the other and broke off the entire top. And there they were.

Mel stared at them a long time, his fears fading slowly. They were certainly alive! One was green, a tiny body of luminous jade, and the other was silkily human-colored, which was why he had been confused on that point. The wings could hardly be anything else, though they were very odd-looking, almost like thin, flexible glass.

He couldn't force himself to touch them. Instead, he laid a folded clean towel on the table and tilted the box very slowly over it. A series of careful tappings and shakings brought the two beings sliding gently out onto the towel.

Two delicately formed female figurines, they lay there a moment, unmoving. Then the green one passed a tiny hand over her forehead in a slow, completely human gesture, opened slanted golden eyes with startled suddenness and looked up at Mel.

He might still have thought he was dreaming, if his attention hadn't been caught just then by a detail of undream-like realism. The other, the human-colored one, seemed to be definitely in a family way.

They were sitting on the folded bath towel in a square of afternoon sunlight which came in through the kitchenette window. The window was high enough up so nobody could look in from outside, and they seemed to want the warmth of the sun more than anything else. They did not appear to be sick, but they were still rather languid. It wasn't starvation, apparently. Mel had put bits of a variety of foods on a napkin before them, and he changed the samples as soon as his guests indicated they weren't interested. So far, canned sardine was the only item that had attracted them at all, and they hadn't done much more than test that.

Between moments of just marveling at them, assuring himself they were there and not an illusion, and wondering *what* they were then and where they'd come from, Mel was beginning to get worried again. For all he knew, they might suddenly die on the bath towel.

"Miss Green," he said in a very low voice—he didn't want to give Maria de Guesgne any indication he was in the house—"I wish you could tell me what you like to eat!"

Miss Green looked up at him and smiled. She was much more alert and vivacious than the other one who, perhaps because of her condition, merely sat or lay there gracefully and let Miss Green wait on her. The relationship seemed to be about that of an elf princess and her personal attendant, but they were much too real-seeming creatures to have popped out of a fairy tale, though their appearance did arouse recurrent bursts of a feeling of fairy tale unreality, which Mel hadn't known since he was ten. But, tiny as they were, Miss Green and the princess primarily gave him the impression of being quite as functional as human beings or, perhaps, as field mice.

He would have liked to inspect the brittle-seeming wings more closely. They seemed to be made up of numerous laminated, very thin sections, and he wondered whether they could fly with them or whether their race had given up or lost that ability.

But touching them might have affected their present matter-of-fact acceptance of him, and he didn't want to risk that....

A door banged suddenly in the apartment overhead. A moment later, he heard Maria coming down the hall stairs.

Mel stood up in sudden alarm. He'd known for some time that his neighbor had supplied herself with a key to his apartment, not to pry but with the practical purpose of borrowing from the little bar in Mel's living room when she was out of both money and liquor. She rarely took much, and until now he'd been more amused than annoyed.

He went hurriedly into the living room, closing the door to the kitchenette behind him. If Maria knocked, he wouldn't answer. If she decided he was out and came in to steal his liquor, he would pretend to have been asleep in the chair and scare the hell out of her!

She paused before the apartment door a moment, but then went out into the court.

Mel waited until her footsteps died away, going toward the street. As he opened the door to the kitchenette, something buzzed noisily out of the living room past his shoulder—a big, unlovely looking horsefly. The apartment screens didn't fit too well, and the fly probably had been attracted by the smell of food.

Startled, he stopped to consider the new problem. There was a flyswatter hanging beside the door, but he didn't want to alarm his guests—and then, for the first time, he saw Miss Green's wings unfold!

She was up on her feet beside the princess, who remained sitting on the towel. Both of them were following the swift, erratic course of the big fly with more animation than they'd shown about anything so far.

Miss Green gave a sudden piping cry, and the glassy appendages on her back opened out suddenly like twin transparently gleaming fans, and blurred into motion too swift for Mel to follow.

Miss Green rose into the air like a tiny human helicopter, hands up before her as if she were praying.

It wasn't till the horsefly swerved from the kitchenette window and came buzzing back that Mel guessed her purpose.

There was a sharper, fiercer drone like a hornet's song as she darted sideways into the insect's path. Mel didn't see her catch it. Its buzzing simply stopped, and then she was dropping gently back to the towel, with the ugly black thing between her hands. It looked nearly as big as her head.

There was an exchange of cheerful piping cries between the two. Miss Green laughed up at Mel's stupefied face, lifted the motionless fly to her mouth and neatly bit off its head.

Mel turned hurriedly and went into the living room. It wasn't, he told himself, really so *very* different from human beings eating a chicken. But he didn't feel up to watching what he knew was going to be a dismemberment and a feast.

At any rate, the horsefly had settled the feeding problem. His guests could take care of themselves.

That night, Miss Green hunted down a few moths. Mel woke up twice with the sudden sharp drone in his ears that told him she had just made her catch. Both times, it was a surge of unthinking physical fright that actually roused him. Awake, and remembering the disproportion in size between himself and the huntress, his reaction seemed ridiculous; but the second time he found he was reluctant to go back to sleep until it would appear that Miss Green was done with her foraging.

So he lay awake, listening to the occasional faint indications of her continuing activity within his apartment, and to more familiar sounds without. A train rattled over a crossing; a police siren gave a sudden view halloo and faded into silence again. For a long time, there was only the whispering passage of distant cars over wet pavements, and the slow roll and thump of the surf. A haze of fog beyond the window turned the apartment into a shut-off little world of its own.

Miss Green moved about with no more than a whisper of air and the muted pipe of voices from the top of the kitchenette cupboard to show where she was. Mel had put a small carton up there, upholstered with the towel and handkerchiefs and roofed over with his best woolen sweater, to make a temporary home for his guests. The princess hadn't stirred from it since, but Miss Green remained busy.

He started suddenly to find her hovering directly over his bed, vaguely silhouetted against the pale blur of the window. As he stared, she settled down and came to rest on the blanket over his chest, effortlessly as a spider gliding down along its thread. Her wings closed with a faint snap.

Mel raised his head carefully to squint down along the blanket at her. It was the first time either of them had made anything resembling a friendly advance in his direction; he didn't want to commit any blunders.

"Hello," he said quietly.

Miss Green didn't reply. She seemed to be looking up at the window, disregarding him, and he was content to watch her. These strange creatures seemed to have some of the aloofness of cats in their manner, and they might be as easily offended.

She turned presently, walked up over the blanket and perched herself on Mel's pillow, above his head and somewhat to his right. And there she stayed silently. Which seemed catlike, too: the granting of a reserved and temporary companionship. He would not have been too surprised to hear a tiny purring from above his ear. Instead, drowsily and lulled in an odd way by Miss Green's presence, he found himself sinking back into sleep.

It wasn't surprising either that his mind should be filled for a time with vague pictures of her, but when the room about him seemed to have expanded into something like a faintly luminous fish-bowl, he knew he was dreaming. There were others present. They were going somewhere, and he had a sense of concern, which had to do either with their destination or with difficulties in getting there. Then a realization of swift, irrevocable disaster—

There were violent lurchings as the luminosity about him faded swiftly into blackness. He felt a terrible, energy-draining cold, the wet clutch of death itself, then something like a soundless explosion about him and anguished cryings. The motion stopped.

Blackness faded back to gray, but the cold remained. Icy water was pounding down on him now, as if he were fighting his way through a vertical current carrying somebody else. A desperate hunt for refuge—and finding it suddenly, and slipping inside and relaxing into unconsciousness, to wait for the return of warmth and life....

Mel's eyes opened. The room was beginning to lighten with morning. He turned his head slowly to look for Miss Green. She was still there, on the pillow beside his head, watching him; and there was something in her position, in the unwinking golden eyes, even in her curious fluff of blue-white hair, that reminded him now less of a cat than a small lizard.

He didn't doubt that she had somehow enabled him to share the experience that in part explained their presence here. Without thinking he asked aloud "What happened to the others?"

She didn't move, but he was aware of a surge of horrified revulsion. Then before his open eyes for a moment swam a picture of a bleak, rain-beaten beach ... and, just above the waterline, in a cluster of harsh voices, jabbing beaks and beating wings, great gulls were tearing apart a strange jetsam of tiny bodies too weakened to escape—

A small, plaintive crying came from the kitchenette. The picture faded as Miss Green soared into the air to attend to her princess.

Mel breakfasted in the living room, thoughtfully. He couldn't quite understand that luminous vehicle of theirs, or why it should have succumbed to the rain storm of Saturday night, which appeared to be what had happened. But his guests obviously were confronted with the problem of getting back to wherever they'd come from—and he didn't think Miss

Green would have confided in him if he wasn't somehow expected to be helpful in solving the problem.

There was a thump on the sill outside his bedroom window, followed by an annoyed meowing. The gray cat that had been spying on the bird box seemed to suspect he was harboring the refugees. Mel went out into the little courtyard through the back door of the duplex and chased the animal away. The fog, he saw, was thinning out quickly; in an hour or so it would be another clear day.

When he came in, Miss Green fluted a few soft notes, which Mel chose to interpret as gratitude, from the top of the cupboard and withdrew from sight again.

One couldn't think of them, he decided, as being exactly like any creatures of Earth. The cold rain had been very nearly deadly to them, if the memory Miss Green had transmitted to him was accurate—as destructive as it had been to their curious craft. Almost as if it could wash right through them, to drain vital energies from their bodies, while in the merely foggy air of last night she had seemed comfortable enough. It indicated different tolerance spans with more sharply defined limits.

The thought came into his mind:

Venus?

It seemed possible, even if it left a lot to explain. Mel got up in sudden excitement and began to walk about the room. He knew not much was known about the second planet, but he had a conviction of being right. It struck him he might be involved in an event of enormous historical significance.

Then, stopping for a moment before the window, he saw it—

Apparently high in the gray sky overhead, a pale yellow circle moved, much smaller than the sun, but like the disk of the sun seen ghostlike through clouds. Instantly, another part of his dream became clear to him.

He lost his head. "Miss Green! Come here, quick!"

A buzz, the swift drone of wings, and she was beside him, perching on his shoulder. Mel pointed.

She gave a lamenting little cry of recognition. As if it had been a signal, the yellow circle darted sideways in a long streaking slant, and vanished. Miss Green fled to report to the princess, while Mel stayed at the window, and quickly returned to him again. Evidently she was both excited and distressed, and he wondered what was wrong. If that apparition of pale light had been one of their vessels, as her behavior indicated, it seemed probable that its mission was to hunt for survivors of the lost globe.

Miss Green seemed either less sure of that, or less confident that the rescue would be easily effected. Some minutes later, she pointed to a different section of the sky, where the yellow circle—or another very like it—was now moving slowly about. Presently it vanished again, and when it reappeared for the second time, it was accompanied by two others.

Meanwhile, Miss Green might have been transmitting some understanding of the nature of her doubts to Mel, because the ghostly vagrants now gave him an immediate impression of insubstantiality: not space-spanning luminous globes but pictured shapes projected on the air. His theory of interplanetary travelers became suddenly much less probable.

In the next few moments, the concept he was struggling with abruptly completed itself in his mind, so abruptly, in fact, that there was no longer any question that it had originated with Miss Green. The rescue craft Mel thought he was seeing actually were just that.

But the pictures in the sky were only signals to possible survivors that help was approaching. The globes themselves were elsewhere, groping their way blindly and dangerously through strange dimensions that had nothing to do with the ones Mel knew.

And they were still, in some manner his imagination did not even attempt to clarify, very, very "far away."

"I was wondering what you'd done with the bird box," Maria de Guesgne explained. "It's not there in the bush any more!"

Mel told her annoyedly that the bird box had been damaged by the storm, and so he'd thrown it into the incinerator.

"Well," Maria said vaguely, "that's too bad." Her handsome dark eyes were shifting about his living room meanwhile, not at all vaguely. Mel had left the apartment door partly open, and she had walked right in on her way to the market. When she wasn't drinking or working herself up to a bout of creative painting, which seemed to put her into a tranced sort of condition, Maria was a highly observant young woman. The question was now how to get her out of the apartment again before she observed more than he wanted her to.

"How does it happen you're not at work on Monday afternoon?" she inquired, and set her shopping bag down on the armchair.

Keeping one eye on the kitchenette door, Mel explained about his vacation. Miss Green hadn't been in sight for almost an hour; but he wasn't at all sure she mightn't come out to inspect the visitor, and the thought of Maria's probable reactions was unnerving.

"Two weeks?" Maria repeated chattily. "It'll be fun having you around for two weeks—unless you're going off to spend your vacation somewhere else. Are you?"

"No," Mel said. "I'm staying here—"

And at that moment, Miss Green came in through the kitchenette door.

At least, Mel assumed it was Miss Green. All he actually saw was a faint blur of motion. It went through the living room, accompanied by a high-pitched hum, and vanished behind Maria.

"Good Lord!" she cried, whirling. "What's that? *Oh!*" The last was a shrill yelp. "It stung me!"

———————————

Mel hadn't imagined Miss Green could move so fast. Rising and falling with furious menace, the sound seemed to come from all points of the room at once, as Maria darted out of the apartment. Clutching her shopping bag, Mel followed her out hastily and slammed the door behind them. He caught up with Maria in the court.

She was rubbing herself angrily.

"I'm not coming into that apartment again, Mel Armstrong," she announced, "until you've had it fumigated! That thing kept stinging me! What was it, anyway?"

"A wasp, I guess." Mel felt weak with relief. She hadn't really seen anything. "Here's your bag. I'll chase it out."

Maria stalked off, complaining about screens that didn't even protect people against giant wasps.

Mel found the apartment quiet again and went into the kitchenette. Miss Green was poised on the top edge of the cupboard, a gold-eyed statuette of Victory, laughing down at him, the laminated wings spread and raised behind her like iridescent glass fans. Mel looked at her with a trace of uneasiness. She had some kind of small white bundle in her arms, and he wondered whether it concealed the weapon with which she'd stung Maria.

"I don't think you should have done that," he told her. "But she's gone now."

Looking rather pleased with herself, Miss Green glanced back over her shoulder and piped a few questioning notes to the princess. There was a soft reply, and she soared down to the table, folded her wings and knelt to lay the bundle gently down on it. She beckoned to Mel.

Mel's eyes popped as she unfolded the bundle. Perhaps he really shouldn't have been surprised.

He was harboring four guests now—the princess had been safely delivered of twins.

At dusk, Miss Green widened the biggest slit in the bedroom screen a little more and slipped out to do her own kind of shopping, with a section of one of Mel's handkerchiefs to serve as a bag.

Mel left the lights out and stayed at the window. He felt depressed, but didn't quite know why—unless it was that so many odd things had happened since Sunday morning that his mind had given up trying to understand them.

He wasn't really sure now, for example, whether he was getting occasional flash-glimpses of those circular luminous vessels plowing through another dimension somewhere, or whether he was half asleep and imagining it. Usually it was a momentary glow printed on the dark air at the edge of his vision, vanishing before he could really look at it.

He had a feeling they had managed to come a good deal closer during the day. Then he wondered briefly whether other people had been seeing strange light-shapes, too, and what they might have thought the glimpses were.

Spots before their eyes, probably.

Miss Green was back with a soft hum of wings, on the outer window sill, six feet from where he sat. She pushed the knotted scrap of cloth through the screen. There was something inside it now; it caught for a moment on the wires. Mel started up to help, then checked himself, afraid of feeling some bug squirming desperately inside; and while he hesitated, she had shoved it through. She followed it, picked it up again and flew off to the living room. After a moment she returned with the empty cloth and went out again.

She made eight such trips in the next hour, while night deepened outside and then began to lighten as a half-moon shoved over the horizon. Mel must have dozed off several times; at least, he suddenly found himself coming awake, with the awareness that something had just landed with a soft thump on the window sill outside.

It wasn't Miss Green. He saw a chunky shadow at one corner of the window, and caught the faintest glint of green eyes peering into the room. It was the cat from the courtyard.

In the same moment, he heard the familiar faint hum, and Miss Green appeared at the opposite end of the sill.

Afterward, Mel realized he'd simply sat there, stiffening in groggy, sleep-dazed horror, as the cat-shadow lengthened and flowed swiftly toward the tiny humanoid figure. Miss Green seemed to raise both arms over her head. A spark of brilliant blue glowed from her cupped hands and extended itself in an almost invisible thread of fire that stabbed against the cat's forehead. The cat yowled, swung aside and leaped down into the court.

Mel was on his feet, shaking violently, as Miss Green slipped in through the screen. He heard Maria open her window upstairs to peer down into the court, where the cat was making low, angry sounds. Apparently it hadn't been hurt, but no wonder Maria had suspected that afternoon she'd been stung by a wasp! Or that Miss Green's insect victims never struggled, once she had caught them!

He pulled down the shade and stood undecided in the dark, until he heard her piping call from the living room. It was followed by an impatient buzzing about the standing lamp in there, and Mel concluded correctly that he was supposed to turn on the light.

He discovered her on the living room table, sorting out the plunder she had brought back.

It wasn't a pile of electrocuted insects, as he had expected, but a puzzlingly commonplace collection—little heaps of dry sand from the beach, some small white pebbles, and a sizable bundle of thin twigs about two inches in length. Since she was disregarding him, he shifted the lamp over to the table to see what this human-shaped lightning bug from another dimension was going to do next.

That was the way he felt about Miss Green at the moment....

What she did was to transport the twigs in two bundles to the top of the cupboard, where she left them with the princess. Then she came back and began to lay out a thin thread of white sand on the dark, polished surface of the table.

Mel pulled up his armchair, poured himself a glass of brandy, lit a cigarette, and settled down to watch her.

By the time Miss Green indicated to him that she wanted the light turned out again, he had finished his second drink and was feeling rather benevolent. She had used up all her sand, and about a square foot of the table's surface was covered now with a confusingly intricate maze of lines, into which she had placed white pebbles here and there. Some of the lines, Mel noticed, blended into each other, while others stopped abruptly or curved back on themselves. As a decorative scheme, it hardly seemed worthwhile.

"Miss Green," he told her thoughtfully, "I hope it makes sense to you. It doesn't to me."

She piped imperiously, pointing: the light! Mel had a moment of annoyance at the way she was ordering him around in his own apartment.

"Well," he said, "I'll humor you this time."

For a moment after he had pulled the switch, he stood beside the table to let his eyes adjust to the dark. However, they weren't adjusting properly—a patch of unquiet phosphorescent glimmering floated disturbingly within his field of vision, and as the seconds passed, it seemed to be growing stronger.

Suddenly, Mel swore in amazement and bent down to examine the table.

"Now what have you done—?" he began.

Miss Green fluted soothingly at him from the dark and fluttered up to his shoulder. He felt a cool touch against his ear and cheek, and a burst of oddly pleasant tinglings ran over his scalp.

"Stop that!" he said, startled.

Miss Green fluted again, urgently. She was trying to tell him something now, and suddenly he thought he understood.

"All right," he said. "I'll look at it. That's what you want me to do, isn't it?"

Miss Green flew down to the table again, which indicated agreement. Mel groped himself back into the chair and leaned forward to study the curiously glowing design she had created of sand and pebbles.

He discovered immediately that any attempt to see it clearly merely strained his vision. Details turned into vaguely distorted, luminous flickerings when he stared at them, and the whole pale, spidery pattern made no more sense than it had with the light on. She must have some purpose in mind with it, but Mel couldn't imagine what.

Meanwhile, Miss Green was making minor adjustments in his position which Mel accepted without argument, since she seemed to know what she was doing. Small tugs and pushes told him she wanted his hands placed on the table to either side of the design. Mel put them there. His head was to be tilted forward just so. He obliged her again. Then she was back on the table, and the top two-thirds of the pattern vanished suddenly behind a blur.

After a moment, he realized she had opened her wings and blotted that part from his sight.

In the darkness, he fastened his puzzled gaze on the remaining section: a quivering, thinly drawn pattern of blue-white light that faded periodically almost to the limits of visibility and slowly grew up again to what was, by comparison, real brilliance. His head was aching slightly. The pattern seemed to tilt sideways and move upward, as if it were creeping in a slow circle about some pivot-point. Presently, it turned down again to complete the circle and start on another round. By that time, the motion seemed normal.

When a tiny shape of light suddenly ran across the design and vanished again as it reached the other side, Mel was only moderately surprised. The figure had reminded him immediately of Miss Green. After a while, it crossed his field of vision in another direction, and then there were two more....

He seemed to be swimming forward, through the pattern, into an area of similar tiny figures like living silhouettes of light, and of entrancingly delicate architectural designs. It was like a marionette setting of incredible craftsmanship, not quite real in the everyday sense, but as convincing as a motion picture which was spreading out, second by second, and beginning to flow about him—

"Hey!" Mel sat up with a start. "You're trying to hypnotize me!"

Miss Green piped pleadingly. Clearly, she had only been trying to show him something. And wasn't it beautiful? Didn't he want to see more?

Mel hesitated. He was suspicious now, but he was also curious. After all, what could she do to him with her tricks?

Besides, he admitted to himself, the picture had vanished as soon as he shifted his eyes, and it *was* beautiful, like moving about through a living illustration of a book of fairy tales.

He yielded. "All right, I do want to see more."

This time, the picture grew up out of the design within seconds. Only it wasn't the same picture. It was as if he had turned around and was looking in another direction, a darker one.

There were fewer of the little light-shapes; instead, he discovered in the distance a line of yellow dots that moved jerkily but steadily, like glowing corks bobbing on dark water. He watched them for a moment without recognition; then he realized with a thrill of pleasure that he was getting another view of the luminous globes he had seen before—this time an other-dimensional view, so to speak.

Suddenly, one of them was right before him! Not a dot or a yellow circle, but a three-foot ball of fire that rushed toward him through the blackness with hissing, sputtering sounds!

Mel surged up out of the chair with a yelp of fright, and the fireball vanished.

As he groped about for the light, Miss Green was piping furiously at him from the table.

Then the light came on.

She was in a rage. Dancing about on the table, beating the air with her wings, she waved her arms over her head and shook her tiny fists at him. Mel backed off warily.

"Take it easy!" he warned. He could reach the flyswatter in the kitchenette with a jump if she started shooting off miniature electric bolts again.

She might have had the same idea, because she calmed down suddenly, shook her wings together and closed them with a snap. It was like a cat smoothing down its bristling back fur. There was a whistling query from the princess now, followed by an excited elfin conversation.

Mel poured himself a drink with a hand that shook slightly, and pretended to ignore the disturbance of his guests, while he tried to figure out what had happened.

Supposing, he thought a trifle guiltily, settling down on the couch at a safe distance from the table—supposing they simply had to have his help at this point. The manner in which one of the rescue globes suddenly had seemed to shift close to him suggested it. Was he justified in refusing to go on with it? In the directionless dark through which the globes were driving, they might have been reacting to his concentrated awareness of them as if it were a radio signal from the human dimensions. And it would explain Miss Green's rage at the sudden interruption of the contact.

But another thought came to him then, and his guilty feelings vanished in a surge of alarmed indignation.

Well, and just supposing, he thought, that he *hadn't* broken the contact. And that a three-foot sputtering fireball materialized right inside his living room!

He caught sight of Miss Green eying him speculatively and rather slyly from the table. She seemed composed enough now; there was even the faintest of smiles on that tiny face. The smile seemed to confirm his suspicions.

Mel downed his drink and stood up.

"Miss Green," he told her evenly, choosing his words with care, "I'm sorry to disappoint you, but I don't intend to be the subject of any more of your experiments. At least not until I've had time to think about it."

Her head nodded slightly, as if she were acknowledging his decision. But the smile remained; in fact, Miss Green had begun to look rather smug. Mel studied her uneasily. She might be planning to put something else over on him, but he knew how to stop that!

Before he turned out the light and went to bed, Mel methodically and somewhat grimly swallowed four more shots of brandy. With that much inside him, it wouldn't matter what Miss Green tried, because he wouldn't be able to react to her suggestions till he woke up again in the morning.

Actually it was noon before he awoke—and he might have gone on sleeping then if somebody hadn't been banging on his apartment door.

"Wake up, Mel!" he heard Maria de Guesgne shouting hoarsely. "I can hear you snoring in there!"

He sat up a little groggily and looked at the clock. His guests weren't in sight.

"You awake, Mel?" she demanded.

"Wait a minute!" he yelled back. "Just woke up and I'm not decent."

When he opened the door, she had vanished. He was about to close it quietly and gratefully again, when she called down the stairway. "That you, Mel? Come on up! I want to show you something."

He locked the door behind him and went upstairs. Maria received him beamingly in her living room. She was on one of her rare creative painting sprees, and this spree, to judge by the spattered appearance of the room and the artist, was more riotous than usual. A half dozen fair-sized canvases were propped on newspapers against the wall to dry. They were turned around, to increase the shock effect on Mel when he would get his first look at them.

"Ever see a salamander?" Maria inquired with anticipation, spreading a few more papers on the table.

Mel admitted he hadn't. He wished she'd given him time to have coffee first. His comments at these private showings were usually regarded as inadequate anyway.

"Well," Maria invited triumphantly, selecting one of the canvases and setting it abruptly up on the table before him, "take a look at one!"

Mel gasped and jerked back. "Holy Judas!" he said in a weak voice.

"Pretty good, eh?" For once, Maria appeared satisfied with his reaction. She held it away from her and regarded it. "One of my best!" she cried judiciously.

About three times life-size, it was a quite recognizable portrait of Miss Green.

It didn't occur to Maria to offer Mel coffee but he got a cigarette from her. Fortunately, he wasn't called upon to make any more comments; she chattered away while she showed him the rest of the series. Mel looked and listened, still rather shaken. Presently he began to ask questions.

A salamander, he learned, was a fire elemental. Maria glanced at her fireplace as she explained this, and Mel noticed she seemed to have had a fire burning there overnight, which wasn't too unusual for her even in the middle of summer. Listening to the bang-haired, bright-eyed oddball rattling off metaphysical details about salamanders, he became aware of a sort of dread growing up in him. For Miss Green was pictured, wings and arms spread, against and within furling veils of yellow-white flame...

"Drawn from life?" he inquired, grinning to make it a joke. He pointed at the picture.

Without looking directly at her, he saw Maria start at the question. She stared at him intensely for a moment, and after that she became more reticent.

It didn't matter because it was all on the canvases. She had seen as much as he had and more, and put it down with shocking realism. Seen through somebody else's eyes, Miss Green's world was still beautiful; but now it was also frightening. And there was what Maria had said about salamanders.

"Maria," he said, "what actually happened last night?"

She looked at him sullenly. "I don't know what you're talking about, Mel."

"I imagine," he suggested casually, "you were just sitting there in front of the fire. And then—"

"Gosh, Mel, she was beautiful! It's *all* so beautiful, you know ..." She recovered quickly. "I fell asleep and I had a dream, that's all. Why? What makes you ask?"

She was beginning to look rather wild-eyed, but he had to find out. "I was just wondering," he said, "whether they'd left."

"Why should they leave—Look, you oaf! I called you in to give you the privilege of looking at my paintings. Now get out. I've got to make a phone call."

He stopped at the door, struck by a sudden suspicion. "You're not going to try to sell them, are you?"

"*Try* to sell them!" She laughed hoarsely. "There are circles, Mel Armstrong, in which a de Guesgne original is *understood*, shall we say? Circles not exactly open to the common herd ... This series," she concluded, rather prosaically, "will get me two thousand bucks as soon as I let one or two of the right people have a look at them!"

Brewing himself a pot of coffee at last, Mel decided that part of it, if true, wasn't any of his business. He had always assumed Maria was living on a monthly check she got from an unidentified source in Chicago, but her occasional creations might have a well-heeled following, at that. As for the way Miss Green had got in to sit for her portrait—the upstairs screens weren't in any better shape than the downstairs ones. The fiery background, of course, might have been only in Maria's mind.

There was a scratching on top of the cupboard and whispery voices. Mel ignored the slight chill that drifted down his spine. Up to that moment, he'd been hoping secretly that Maria had provided a beacon for the rescue team to home in on while he slept, and that his guests had been picked up and taken home.

But Miss Green was peering down at him over the edge of the cupboard.

"Hi, salamander!" he greeted her politely. "Had a busy night? Too bad it didn't work."

Her head withdrew. In the living room Mel stopped to look at the design of sand and pebbles, which was still on the table. Touching one of the threadlike lines, he discovered it was as hard and slick as lacquer. Otherwise the pattern seemed unremarkable in daylight, but Mel dropped a cloth across it to keep it out of sight.

Miss Green fluttered past him to the sill of the bedroom window. He watched her standing on tiptoe against the screen, apparently peering about at the sky. After a while, it began to seem ridiculous to let himself become obsessed by superstitious fears about this tiny and beautiful, almost jewellike creature. Whatever abilities she might have, she and the princess were only trying to get home—and, having seen their home, he couldn't blame them for that.

He had a return of the fairy-tale nostalgia his glimpse of those eerily beautiful places had aroused in him the night before, a pleasantly yearning sensation like an awareness of elfin horns blowing far away to send faint, exciting echoes swirling about the commonplace sky of Sweetwater Bay. The feeling might have been resurrected from his childhood, but it was a strong and effective one.

He recalled how bored he'd been with everything before they appeared ...

He walked softly through the bedroom and stopped behind Miss Green. She was making an elaborate pretense of not having noticed his approach, but the pointed ears that could follow the passage of a moth in the dark were tilted stiffly backward. Mel actually was opening his mouth to say, "Miss Green, I'll help you if I can," when it struck him sharply, like a brand-new thought, that it was an extremely rash promise to make, considering everything that had happened so far.

He wondered how the odd impulse ever had come to him.

In sudden suspicion, he began to trace the last few minutes through again. He had started with a firm decision not to let his guests involve him in their plans any more than was healthy for him, if at all—and the decision had been transformed, step by step, and mental twist by mental twist, into a foolish willingness to have them make use of him exactly as they pleased!

Miss Green, still maliciously pretending to watch the sky, let him think it all out until it became quite clear what she had done and how she had done it. And then, as Mel spluttered angrily at this latest interference with his freedom of thought and action, she turned around and laughed at him.

In a way, it cleared the air. The pressure was off. Maria had proved a much more pliable subject than Mel; the rescuers had their bearings and would arrive presently. Meanwhile, everybody could relax.

Mel couldn't help feeling relieved as he grew sure of that. At the same time, now that the departure was settled, he became aware of a certain amount of belated regret. Miss Green didn't seem to know the exact hour; she was simply watching for them well ahead of their arrival.

Where would they show up? She waved her arms around in an appealingly helpless gesture at the court outside and the sky. Here, there—somewhere in the area.

It would be a fire globe. At his question, she pointed at the opposite wall of the court where a picture of one formed itself obligingly, slid along the wall a few feet, and vanished. Mel was beginning to enjoy all this easy last-minute communication, when he heard Maria come downstairs and open the door to the other court. There was conversation, and several sets of footsteps went up to her apartment and down again.

Cautioning Miss Green, he took a look around the shutters of the living room window. A small panel truck stood in the court; Maria was supervising the careful transfer of her paintings into its interior. Apparently she didn't even intend to let them dry before offering them for sale!

The truck drove off with Maria inside with her paintings, and Mel discovered Miss Green doing a little spying of her own from the upper edge of the shutters. Good friends now, they smiled at each other and resumed their guard at the bedroom window.

The princess joined them around five in the afternoon. Whether she had been injured in the accident or weakened by the birth of her babies, Mel couldn't tell, but Miss Green carried her friend down from the cupboard without visible effort, and then went back for a globular basket of tightly woven tiny twigs, which contained the twins.

It was a masterfully designed little structure with a single opening about the thickness of a pencil, and heavily lined. Mel had a notion to ask for it as a souvenir, but decided against it. He lifted it carefully to his ear, to listen to an almost inaudible squeaking inside, and his expression seemed to cause Miss Green considerable silent amusement.

All in all, it was much like waiting patiently in pleasant company for the arrival of an overdue train. Then, around seven o'clock, when the room was already dark, the telephone rang abruptly and returned Mel with a start to the world of human beings.

He lifted the receiver.

"Hello, oaf!" said Maria de Guesgne in what seemed for the moment to be an enormous, booming voice.

Mel inquired agreeably whether she'd succeeded in selling her paintings. It was the first thing that occurred to him.

"Certainly I sold them!" Maria said. He could tell by now that she was thoroughly plastered again. "Got a message to give you," she added.

"From whom?"

"Maybe from me, ha-ha!" said Maria. She paused a moment, seemed to be muttering something to herself, and resumed suddenly, "Oaf, are you listening?"

Mel said bluntly that he was. If he hung up on her, she would probably ring back.

"All right," Maria said clearly. "This is the message: 'The fiery ones do not tolerate the endangering of their secrets.' Warning, see? Goo'-bye."

She hung up before he could say anything.

Hers had been a chilling sort of intrusion. Mel stood a while in the darkening room, trying to gather up the mood Maria had shattered, and discovering he couldn't quite do it. He realized that all along, like a minor theme, there had been a trace of fear underlying everything he did, ever since he had first looked into that bird box and glimpsed something impossible inside it. He had been covering the fear up; even now he didn't want to admit it, but it was there.

He could quite simply, of course, walk out of the room and out of the apartment, and stay away for a week. He didn't even ever have to come back. And, strictly speaking, this was the sort of thing that should have happened to somebody like Maria de Guesgne, not to him. For him, the sensible move right now would be to go quietly back into the normal world of reality he had stepped out of a few mornings ago. It was a simple physical act. The door was over there...

Then Mel looked back at his guests and promptly reversed his decision. They were certainly as real as any living creatures he'd ever seen, and he felt

- 23 -

there weren't many human beings who would show up as well as Miss Green had done in any comparable emergency. His own unconscious fears meant only that he had run into a new and unpredictable factor in a world that had been becoming increasingly commonplace for a number of years now. He could see that once you'd got settled into the idea of a commonplace world, you might be startled by discoveries that didn't fit that notion—and he felt now, rather hazily, that it wasn't such a bad thing to be startled like that. It might wake you up enough to let you start living again yourself.

He took the receiver off the phone and laid it on the floor, so there wouldn't be any more interruptions. If he ran off now before seeing how the adventure ended, he knew he would never quit regretting it.

He went into the bedroom and pulled his chair back up to the window. The shadowy silhouette that was Miss Green turned and sounded a few fluting notes at him. He had the immediate impression that she was worried.

What was the matter?

She pointed.

Clouds!

The sky was still full of the pastel glowings of the sunset. Here and there were patches of black cloud, insignificant-looking, like ragged crows swimming through the pale light.

"*Rain*," the thought came. "*The cold rain—the killing rain! Another storm!*"

Mel studied the sky uneasily. They might be right. "Your friends are bound to get here first," he assured them, looking confident about it.

They smiled gratefully at him. He couldn't think of anything he might do to help. The princess looked comfortable on the towel he had laid along the screen, and Miss Green, as usual, looked alert, prepared to handle anything that had to be handled. He wondered about asking her to let him see how the globes were doing, and, instantly, a thought showed clear in his mind: "*Try it yourself!*"

That hadn't occurred to Mel before. He settled back comfortably in the chair and looked through the screen for them.

Four or five fiery visualizations quivered here and there in the air, vanished, reappeared, vanished ...

Mel stopped looking for them, and there was only the sky.

"Closer?" he said aloud, rather pleased with himself. It had been easy!

Miss Green nodded, human fashion, and piped something in reply. Closer, but—

He gathered she couldn't tell from here how close, and that there was trouble—a not quite translatable kind of trouble, but almost as if, in *their* dimension, they were struggling through the radiant distortions of a storm that hadn't gathered yet here on Earth.

He glanced up at the sky again, more anxiously now. The black clouds didn't seem to have grown any larger.

By and by, because he had not had any awareness of going to sleep, Mel was surprised to find himself waking up. He knew immediately that he had been asleep a long time, a period of hours. There was grayness around him, the vague near-light of very early morning, and he had a sense of having been aroused by a swirling confusion of angry sounds. But all was silent at the moment.

Her answer was instantly in his mind. The storm had caused a delay—but a great globe was almost here now!

A curious pause followed. Mel had a sense of hesitation. And then, very swiftly and faintly, a wisp of thought, which he would have missed if that pause had not made him alert, showed and vanished on the fringe of his consciousness:

"*Be careful! Be very careful.*"

Miss Green turned back to the window. Beside her now, Mel saw the princess sitting as if asleep, with one arm across the twig basket and her head resting on her arm. Before he could frame the puzzled question that was struggling up in his mind, there was a series of ear-splitting yowls from the court outside. It startled Mel only for a moment, since it was a familiar sort of racket. The gray cat didn't tolerate intruding felines in its area, and about once a month it discovered and evicted one with the same lack of inhibition it was evidencing right now. It must have been the threatening squalls which usually preceded the actual battle that had awakened him.

The encounter itself was over almost instantly. There were sounds of a scampering retreat which ended beyond the garage, and, standing up at the window, Mel saw the gray shape of the winner come gliding back down the court. The cat stopped below him and seemed to turn up its head. For a moment, he felt it was staring both at him and at Miss Green, very much like a competent little tiger in the gusty, gray night; then it made a low, menacing sound and moved on out of sight. Apparently it hadn't yet forgotten its previous meeting with Miss Green.

Mel looked down at her. "Why should I be careful?"

There was a pause again, and what came then hardly seemed an answer to his question. The princess was very weak, Miss Green indicated; he might have to help.

He was still wondering about that—and wondering, too, whether he'd really had something like a warning from her—when a sudden wavering glare lit up the room behind them!

For a moment, he thought the fireball was inside the building. But the light was pouring in through the living room window; its source was in the opposite court, out of his line of sight. There was a crackling, hissing sound, and the light faded.

Miss Green came darting at him. Mel put his hand up instinctively and felt her thrust the basket into it. Almost instantly, she had picked up the princess and was outside the screen—

Then the cat attacked from below in a silent, terrible leap, a long, twisting shadow in the air, and they seemed to drop out of sight together.

Mel was out in the court, staring wildly around. In the swimming grayness nothing stirred or made sound. A cool, moist wind thrust at his face and faded. Except for the toy basket of twigs in his hand, he might have been awakening from a meaningless dream.

Then a lurid round of light like a big, wavering moon came out over the top of the building, and a sharp humming sound drove down through the air at him. Instinctively again, he held out the basket and felt it plucked away. He thought it was Miss Green, but the shape had come and gone much too swiftly to be sure of that.

The light grew brilliant, a solid white—intolerable—and he backed hurriedly into the shelter of the garage, his heart hammering in excitement and alarm. He heard voices from the other court; a window slammed somewhere. He couldn't guess what was happening, but he didn't need Miss Green's warning now. He had an overwhelming urge to keep out of sight until the unearthly visitor would be gone—

And then, running like a rabbit, the gray cat appeared from behind a box halfway down the court and came streaking for the garage. Mel watched its approach with a sort of silent horror, partly because it might be attracting undesirable attention to him—and partly because he seemed to know in that instant exactly what was going to be done to it.

It wasn't more than twenty feet away when something like a twisting string of fiery white reached down from above. The animal leaped sideways, blazed and died. There was a sound very like a gunshot, and the court was instantly dark.

Mel stayed where he was. For half a minute or so, he was shaking much too violently to have left his retreat. By the end of that time, he knew better. It wasn't over yet!

Pictures forming in the moist, dark air ... delicate, unstable outlines sliding through the court, changing as they moved. Elfin castles swayed up out of grayness and vanished again. Near the edge of his vision other shapes showed, more beautiful than human...

Muttering to himself, between terror and delight, Mel closed his eyes as tightly as he could, which helped for a moment. But then the impressions began drifting through his mind. The visitors were still nearby, hanging somewhere outside the limits of human sight in their monstrous fireball, in the windy sky. They were talking to him in their way.

Mel asked in his mind what they wanted, and the answer showed immediately. The table in his living room with the pattern of glassy sand and pebbles Miss Green had constructed. The pattern was glowing again now under the cloth he had thrown over it. He was to go in and look at the pattern ...

"No!" he said aloud. It was all terror now.

"Go look at the pattern ... Go look at the pattern ..."

The pictures burst round him in a soundless wild flowering of beauty, flickering rains of color, a fountain of melting, shifting forms. His mind drowned in happiness. He was sinking through a warmth of kindness, gratitude and love...

A drift of rain touched his cheek coldly—and Mel found himself outside the garage, moving drunkenly toward the apartment door. Then, just for a moment, a picture of Miss Green printed itself on his mind.

She seemed to be standing before him, as tall now as he was, motionless, the strange wings half spread. The golden unhuman eyes were looking past him, watching something with cold malice and contempt—and with a concentration of purpose that made a death's mask of the perfectly chiseled green face!

In that second, Mel understood the purpose as clearly as if she had told him. In the next, the image disappeared with a jerky, complete abruptness—

As if somebody were belatedly trying to wipe it out of his memory as well! But he knew he had seen her somehow—somewhere—as she actually was at that moment. And he knew what she had been watching. Himself, Mel Armstrong, staggering blindly about in his other-dimension, down in the court!

He hadn't stayed in the court. He was back in the garage, backed trembling against a wall. She—*they*—weren't trying to show him gratitude, or reward him somehow; before they left, they simply wanted to destroy the human being who had found out about them, and whom they had used. The table and the pattern were some sort of trap! What he couldn't understand was why they didn't simply come down in their fireball and kill him as they had the cat.

They were still pouring their pictures at him, but he knew now how to counteract that. He stared out through the garage window at the lightening sky—looked at, listened to, what was there, filling his mind with Earth shapes and sounds!

And he promptly discovered an ally he hadn't been counting on. He hadn't really been aware of the thumping wind before, and the sketchy pattering of raindrops, like a sweeping fall of leaves here and there. He hadn't even heard, beyond the continuous dim roar of surf from the beach, the gathering mutter of thunder!

They couldn't stay here long. The storm was ready to break. They weren't willing to risk coming out fully into the Earth dimension to hunt him down. And he didn't have to go to their trap ...

Rain spattered louder and closer. The sweat chilled on Mel's body as his breathing grew quieter. They hadn't left him yet. If he relaxed his eyes and his mind, there was an instant faint recurrence of the swirling unearthly patterns. But he could keep them out by looking at what was really here. He only had to wait—

Then the rain came down in a great, rushing tide, and he knew they were gone.

———————————

For a few seconds, he remained where he was, weak with relief. Over the noise of the storm, he heard human voices faintly from the other court and from neighboring houses. That final crash must have awakened

- 28 -

everybody—and someone had seen the great globe of fire when it first appeared.

There should be some interesting gossip in the morning!

Which concerned Mel not at all. After drinking in the sweet certainty of being still alive and safe, he had become aware of an entirely unexpected emotion, which was, curiously, a brief but sharp pang of grief at Miss Green's betrayal. Why, he must have been practically in love with that other-dimensional, human-shaped rattlesnake! Mulling it over in moody amazement at himself, it struck Mel suddenly then that one could interpret her final action somewhat differently, too.

Because she could have planted that apparently revealing picture of herself deliberately in his mind, to stop him from stumbling into the trap the others had set for him! She might have been planning to save him from the beginning, or merely relented at the last moment. There was no way of ever really knowing now, but Mel found he preferred to believe that Miss Green's intention was good.

In the driving rain, he hesitated a moment beside the blackened lump that had been the cat, but he couldn't force himself to pick it up and remove it. If someone else found it, it might add to the gossip, but that wasn't any business of his any more. Everyone knew that lightning did funny, selective things. So far as he was concerned, the matter was all over.

He opened the duplex door and stood staring.

His apartment door was open and the room beyond was dark, as he had left it. But down the little stairway and out of Maria's upstairs apartment, light poured in a quiet flood.

She must have returned during the night while he was sleeping, probably drunk as a hoot-owl. The commotion downstairs hadn't been enough to arouse her. But something else had—she'd come down following swirling, beautiful, unearthly pictures, hunting the pattern that would guide her straight into a promised delight!

Mel didn't have to reach into the apartment to switch on the light. Lightning did funny, selective things, all right, and from where he stood, he could smell what had happened. They hadn't wasted that final bolt, after all!

Oddly enough, what was uppermost in his mind in those seconds, while he continued to put off seeing what he was going to have to look at very soon, was the final awareness of how he must have appeared in their eyes:

A stupid native, barely capable of receiving training and instruction enough to be a useful servant. Beyond that, they had simply had no interest in him.

It was Maria they had worried about. The mental impressions he'd picked up in the court had been directed at her. Miss Green had been obliged to stop him finally from springing a trap which was set for another.

For Maria, who might have endangered their leaving.